Dear Parents:

Congratulations! Your child is taking the first steps on an exciting journey. The destination? Independent reading!

STEP INTO READING® will help your child get there. The program offers five steps to reading success. Each step includes fun stories and colorful art or photographs. In addition to original fiction and books with favorite characters, there are Step into Reading Non-Fiction Readers, Phonics Readers and Boxed Sets, Sticker Readers, and Comic Readers—a complete literacy program with something to interest every child.

Learning to Read, Step by Step!

Ready to Read   Preschool–Kindergarten
• big type and easy words • rhyme and rhythm • picture clues
For children who know the alphabet and are eager to begin reading.

Reading with Help   Preschool–Grade 1
• basic vocabulary • short sentences • simple stories
For children who recognize familiar words and sound out new words with help.

Reading on Your Own   Grades 1–3
• engaging characters • easy-to-follow plots • popular topics
For children who are ready to read on their own.

Reading Paragraphs   Grades 2–3
• challenging vocabulary • short paragraphs • exciting stories
For newly independent readers who read simple sentences with confidence.

Ready for Chapters   Grades 2–4
• chapters • longer paragraphs • full-color art
For children who want to take the plunge into chapter books but still like colorful pictures.

STEP INTO READING® is designed to give every child a successful reading experience. The grade levels are only guides; children will progress through the steps at their own speed, developing confidence in their reading.

Remember, a lifetime love of reading starts with a single step!

Visit us on the Web!
StepIntoReading.com
rhcbooks.com

Educators and librarians, for a variety of teaching tools, visit us at RHTeachersLibrarians.com

ISBN 978-0-593-37372-9 (trade) — ISBN 978-0-593-37373-6 (lib. bdg.)

Printed in the United States of America

10 9 8 7 6 5 4 3 2 1

2021 Edition

STEP INTO READING®

2

STEP

READING WITH HELP

nickelodeon

BACK ON TRACK!

PAW PATROL THE MOVIE™

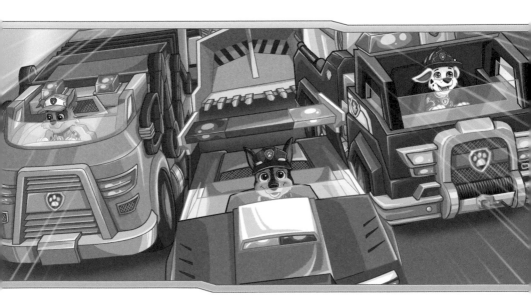

by Christy Webster

illustrated by Nate Lovett

Random House 🏠 New York

The PAW Patrol
is in Adventure City.
The mayor has
built a train track
with big loops!

A subway car

speeds toward the loops.

The car
gets stuck!

The PupPad rings.

The caller is upside down!

They need help.

The PAW Patrol

is on the roll!

Skye flies high.
She will save
the train!

The loop sways.
It might fall!
Rocky uses his truck
to hold it up.

The loop is still tipping!
Rocky's truck cannot
hold it.

Skye dives through the loop.

She wraps a cable around it.

Skye lifts the loop.

The car is safe!

But the people

are still stuck inside.

Rubble dumps cement.

Marshall takes aim.

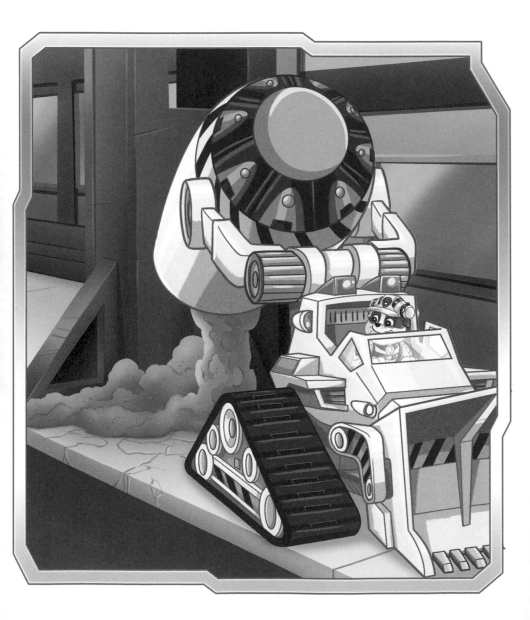

Marshall shoots
a huge ladder out
of his fire truck.
It leans against
the loop.

The people open
the subway door.
They look down.
They are very high up!
Marshall hits a switch.

The ladder turns into a slide!

Everyone is safe.

Good job, pups!